Lyra and Bon Bon

✳✳* and *✳*✳*

the Mares from S.M.I.L.E.

By G. M. Berrow

Little, Brown and Company
New York Boston

HASBRO and its logo, MY LITTLE PONY and all related characters are trademarks of Hasbro and are used with permission. © 2016 Hasbro. All Rights Reserved.

Little, Brown and Company

Hachette Book Group
1290 Avenue of the Americas, New York, NY 10104
lb-kids.com

Little, Brown and Company is a division of Hachette Book Group, Inc.
The Little, Brown name and logo are trademarks of Hachette Book Group, Inc.

The publisher is not responsible for websites (or their content) that are not owned by the publisher.

First Edition: March 2016

Library of Congress Control Number: 2016930093

ISBN 978-0-316-31217-2

10 9 8 7 6 5 4 3 2 1

RRD-C

Printed in the United States of America

For all the pony fans—you're not just in the background.

CONTENTS

★ ★ ★

Chapter 1

Hearts and Hooves

★ ★ ★

"Thanks for going with me to the party, Bon Bon," said Lyra as she followed her best friend into the cottage. Lyra, a mint-green Unicorn, broke into a tiny smile.

"It was nothing, really," replied Bon Bon, distracted. She trotted around the room, looking under furniture and opening closets.

"Stop." Lyra put her hoof on Bon Bon's shoulder and caught her eye. "It meant a lot to me. I know how you despise social events like that, even when they are thrown by Ponyville's best party planner—Pinkie Pie."

Lyra reflected on the party, riffling through the snapshots in her mind of fun Hearts and Hooves Day activities. There had been cards, songs, heart-shaped confetti, and chocolate treats as far as the eye could see. They had played a game where everypony tried to guess the new filling flavors of the truffles that Pinkie Pie had whipped up especially for the party. Bon Bon had won by guessing "caramarshmallow sprinkle," but seemed quite embarrassed about it—she had demanded they make a quick exit right after.

"The party was fine, but I just don't enjoy small talk like you do, Lyra." Bon Bon sighed deeply as she latched the double lock on the door. Her eyes darted to the front window. The curtains were pushed aside, letting the daylight stream in. She suppressed the urge to canter over and close them immediately. Lyra preferred a bright cottage when she visited. "I'm a product of my past, it seems. No personal details allowed."

Lyra giggled. "You mean your *secret* past as one of Equestria's top monster-fighting secret agents?"

"Shhhh!" Bon Bon hissed as she looked around the small, unoccupied room. "They could have it bugged," Bon Bon barked. "Somepony is *always* listening."

"Sorry, I forgot." Lyra rolled her eyes. "But you're being a little bit paranoid. Besides, all that secret monster stuff is behind you now!"

"Where?" Bon Bon whipped around.

Lyra rolled her eyes again. "Can we just move on to our own Hearts and Hooves Day tradition now?"

"Hearts and Hooves frozen hot cocoa? Sure. Yeah, good idea." The two ponies trotted to the kitchen. *Maybe Lyra is right,* thought Bon Bon. She really needed to calm down. Nopony (or monster) was out to get her. She was safe here in Ponyville, living her simple life and watching her best buddy whip up a yummy treat.

Bon Bon plopped down at the dining table and took a deep breath. *Act normal,* she told herself. *You did before Lyra found out the truth.* "I'm surprised you want to have any more chocolate today!"

"There's no such thing as too much

chocolate." Lyra opened the icebox and began to prepare the beverages.

"I'm so glad you taught me how to make this. Where did you find the recipe?" asked Lyra. She used her magic to pour chocolate syrup into a mixing bowl. "I always forget!"

"At the agency actually." Bon Bon grinned, recalling the day. "The gang and I were doing some experiments with cryogenic freezing when somepony accidentally zapped the cocoa pot in the corner! Produced the most delicious drink ever." Bon Bon laughed. "We tried to replicate it, but only the Unicorns on the team could do it. So we came up with this version, which doesn't require a freeze zap. Just ice and a good shaker."

"You told me you learned it at college!"

Lyra teased. She shook the ice and chocolate around in the shaker. It rattled noisily. "I swear, Bon Bon. It's like getting to know you all over again...."

Bon Bon looked down at her hooves. *Poor Lyra.*

"Which is kind of awesome," Lyra added with a wink.

Bon Bon breathed a sigh of relief. "I'm so lucky to have somepony in my life who is as understanding as you are, Lyra. Even after all the lies."

"Well, I hope things never change!" Lyra replied, passing a frosty mug of frozen hot cocoa to her buddy. The two ponies held up their mugs.

"To being best friends forever!" they cheered in unison.

They had barely clinked their drinks

when a loud knock rattled the door. *Thump, thump, thump!* The commotion nearly knocked it clean off its hinges. *Thump, thump, thump!*

Lyra raised an inquisitive brow. "I'll get it...."

"No!" Bon Bon hissed. She knew that knock. "Whatever you do, stay hidden."

Chapter 2

By Task Force

✶ ✶ ✶

Bon Bon gracefully sprung to her hooves, her pink-and-blue mane billowing out around her face. She shot Lyra a serious look. *Be quiet.*

Thump, thump, thump! The persistent knocking hadn't stopped. By Bon Bon's calculations, there was less than a minute until her cottage was doorless. Creeping from the kitchen, Bon Bon dropped to the living room floor. She silently scooted her way across to the front window and whipped out the tiny hoofheld mirror she kept hidden inside her mane at all times.

Bon Bon leveraged her body weight against the wall, crouching low, and slowly raised the mirror to see who the visitor was. There was a 0.09 percent chance her instincts had failed her, which was enough of a margin of error for her to be extra cautious.

When she saw the Unicorn stallion's bristled face, Bon Bon felt as if the wind had been knocked out of her chest. Even though her mind had been expecting it, she could not prepare herself emotionally for the shock of seeing *him* again. It was Agent Furlong, Bon Bon's hard-muzzled boss from the agency. Her superior from another time, another life than this. What was he doing here in Ponyville?

Whatever the reason for his visit, Bon Bon was still 100 percent sure of one fact. Lyra could not be seen. Not if Bon Bon wanted to keep her dear friend safe.

Thump, thump, thump!

"Special Agent Drops!" Furlong shouted in his scratchy voice. "I'll have you know that knocking is merely a courtesy. I'll enter the premises regardless of whether you open the door." Furlong coughed. "I assume you want to keep your door, Drops!"

"Who is it?" Lyra took a loud slurp of her cocoa, which left an unsightly chocolate mustache on her muzzle. Bon Bon frantically motioned for her to get down. Lyra was right in the sight line of the window! In one swift motion, Bon Bon leaped toward the mint-green Unicorn, pulled her toward the closet, and shoved her inside. "What's going on, Bon—?" Bon Bon heard Lyra's muffled voice shout through the winter coats as she slammed the closet door shut.

WHAM! Bon Bon's door flew off the hinges and collapsed onto the wooden floor in a puff of dust.

"Nice place ya got here, kid," Furlong mused as he trotted in casually as if he hadn't just caused panic in the extreme *and* ruined her front door. "Real quaint. Normal." He turned to her, removed his dark sunglasses, and smoothed down his springy salt-and-pepper mane. "Good cover. It works, kid."

He trotted toward the kitchen and stuck in his nose. Furlong raised his bushy eyebrows but didn't say a word. He just grunted.

"Why are you here?" Bon Bon tried to

sound calm. Her eyes darted to the closet door. She willed Lyra to stay put with the power of her mind. "Just passing through on the way to your deep-cover identity? I heard they were gonna set you up real nice for your retirement."

Agent Furlong frowned. "I'm not that old, kid." Furlong coughed again. He was scarily close to where Lyra was hiding.

Bon Bon trotted over and put a hoof on his shoulder. She led him back toward the middle of the room. "What happened to 'a beach hut and pineapple smoothies for the rest of my days'?"

"I've still got fight left in me." Furlong made a strange face and coughed a third time. "Besides, *I was bored.*" He took off his black blazer and started toward the closet again.

"Let me take that for you!" Bon Bon swiped the jacket and hung it on the back of an armchair. Furlong tilted his head in a way that used to make Bon Bon nervous. He knew. She was sure of it.

"Would you like some tea?" Bon Bon asked, her voice wavering. "Or some frozen hot cocoa! I just made some like the old days—"

"Look, kid. I'm not gonna sit here and make nice. I'm gonna cut to the chase. We need you back on the squad." Furlong smiled. "We leave tonight."

Chapter 3

True Lyras

★ ★ ★

"But…" Bon Bon shook her head. "The squad has been disbanded! The whole operation in Canterlot shuttered after the incident with the bugbear—"

"*That* branch of the operation was." Furlong nodded, solemn. "But the agency lives on."

"There's another branch?" She plopped down on her velvet sofa in disbelief. Bon

Bon tried to wrap her head around this news, but she just couldn't seem to do it. "Where?"

"You know full well I can't say anymore here in Fillyville—"

"It's *Ponyville*," Bon Bon corrected. She stood up, resolute. "And it's my home now. I can't just up and leave like that! I have obligations.... I have a cottage...." Her eyes darted to the closet door. "I have *friends*."

"Well, then my best suggestion is that you forget about them. And fast."

"But I can't—"

Furlong grunted. "Special Agent Drops, you knew what you signed up for." He looked at his agency-issued watch. Standard black band with a silver brushed-steel face. Cold and functional, just like the agency. But he was right. She had made an oath to serve.

"I'll give you a few moments to gather some personal effects, and then we'll be off."

"When will I be able to return to Ponyville?" Bon Bon hung her head. "Is it a long mission?" Perhaps she would return within the week. She could explain everything to Lyra then.

Furlong laughed. "You were always so optimistic, Drops."

"What's that supposed to mean?"

"You're not coming back to Fillyville. This mission is indefinite. And if it does end soon, you'll be reassigned a new deep cover. This one is blown," he said, nodding to the closet. The words hit Bon Bon like a ton of rocks. Leave Ponyville forever? What about her cottage? And her monthly book club? And her favorite lemon cupcakes from

Sugarcube Corner? And what in the world would she do without her confidante, her one true best friend?

"Noooooo!" Lyra called out as she burst from the closet. "You can't do this!"

"Lyra!" Bon Bon shouted. "What are you doing?"

"I'm not going to let you take her away," Lyra said, galloping over to Agent Furlong. He had a stern expression on his face. "She's my best friend in the whole world. You can't just take a pony's *best friend* away!" Lyra's face contorted into a desperate expression.

"Sure, I get it, kid." Agent Furlong looked bored. He blew on his watch and shined it with a small rag from his satchel. "It's emotional and all that." He looked to Bon Bon. "But I don't have time for this, and neither do you."

Bon Bon barely had a moment to think before she saw Furlong whip out his small hoof mirror, same as hers. He pointed its face directly at Lyra. "Now look at the pretty mirror, miss." Purple magic began to glow upon the tip of his horn. Lyra went still, suddenly hypnotized by the shiny mirror.

"Stop!" Bon Bon backflipped across the room, snatching the mirror and crouching low into a graceful pose. She stood up. "If you erase Lyra's memory, she'll forget our whole friendship." Bon Bon looked to Lyra. "I wouldn't be able to bear it."

"Hey, kid, I was just trying to make things easier on you," Agent Furlong replied. "Plus, it's the only option. She knows too much about the agency. Can we get on with it?"

As much as she didn't want to admit it,

Agent Furlong had a point. Why had she allowed herself to get close to Lyra? To put her in harm's way? Bon Bon shielded her eyes. She couldn't bear to watch their shared memories disappear into thin air.

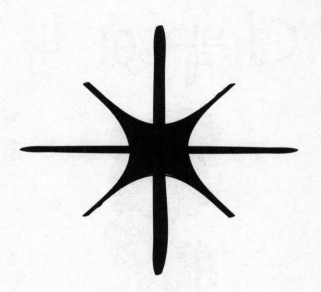

Chapter 4

The Hidequarters

* * *

The three ponies were at a standstill in the living room. Furlong was poised with the mirror in his hoof, yet something was preventing him from moving on with the deed. Lyra was still mesmerized by the gadget, unaware of what hung in the balance. Just *all* her memories about Bon Bon—no big deal!

"Wait!" Bon Bon broke the silence. She trotted in front of Lyra, in turn breaking her gaze from the hoof mirror. "Are you sure there's no other way?"

"I have an idea...but it requires sacrifice." Furlong cocked his head, sizing up the mint-green Unicorn. "A great big one."

"What is it?" Bon Bon said, brightening. Her cerulean eyes grew large. "Whatever it is, I'll do it. For Lyra."

"Not yours, kid. *Hers.*" Furlong gestured at Lyra, who was blinking furiously. She looked quite confused. "If you want Lyra to keep her memories of your friendship, she'll have to join the agency, too." He shrugged as if it were all quite simple. Business as usual. Bon Bon normally liked that quality in him, but right now it annoyed her.

"Join the agency?" Lyra perked up. "Together?"

"Absolutely not!" Bon Bon protested with

a frown. She didn't want to drag Lyra into all of this, too. It was a dangerous life, protecting Equestria from all those monsters.

"You get two seconds to decide, kid." Furlong looked at his watch. "We have to leave *now*."

"Good-bye, Ponyville," whimpered Bon Bon. *So much for the simple life*, she thought, just as Lyra echoed her words much more enthusiastically.

"Good-bye, Ponyville! We're going undercover!"

Lyra gasped as she stepped onto the Hooflyn Bridge, scanning the Manehattan skyline. Tall towers of glass and metal sparkled brilliantly in the midday sunshine. "I forgot how beautiful it was!" Lyra exclaimed as if she were on vacation. Just a tourist here to see the Neighcy's Harvest Balloon Parade and do a bit of shopping on the side. "Look, Bon Bon! It's the Crystaller Building! I can't believe it."

"And I can't believe I didn't know we had a branch of the agency in Manehattan!" Bon Bon said, shaking her head. She was not in the mood to check out Bridleway shows and visit museums. "Makes me wonder what else I don't know, Agent Furlong." Bon Bon raised a suspicious brow.

"Plenty." Furlong grunted. "And that's how it has to be, kid." He looked tired. Maybe he was starting to regret bringing the overenthusiastic Lyra into all this. "Now stay near me and don't talk to anypony." He motioned his hoof at them, and the two mares began to follow across the bridge.

At the other end, a yellow taxi carriage waited for them. Without a word, Furlong hopped in. Lyra and Bon Bon followed suit, and soon they were whisked into the bustling city streets. The cart rattled through the avenues, making sharp turns and speeding through the traffic signals. As they passed the Stockyard Exchange, Lyra bounced along with a silly smile on her face. Bon Bon bit her lip in anxious anticipation. *This is just the beginning of a bumpy ride*, thought Bon Bon.

The carriage came to an abrupt halt in front of a hole-in-the-wall joint called Hay's Pizza. Agent Furlong tossed the driver some bits and hopped out onto the sidewalk.

"Are we stopping for lunch first?" Lyra asked. "'Cause I'm starving!"

"Yes-we-are-getting-some-lunch-now,"

Furlong replied robotically. "Yum-yum." He shot Bon Bon a warning look. She finally understood what was happening. It had to be a secret entrance to the new agency digs! Bon Bon grabbed Lyra and pulled her inside. "Just be quiet 'til we get there, okay? We'll eat later. We have to be discreet."

"Oh, okay...." Lyra said with a whimper. The smells wafting around inside Hay's were so enticing that they made her stomach rumble audibly. A few ponies chowing down on huge, cheesy slices of broccoli pizza looked up at them. She reached her hoof around her tummy to silence it.

They stopped at the front counter. "We're here for our shift, Sauce!" Furlong called out to a red pony with a tomato cutie mark.

"Ah, right on time. The dough needs kneading in back." He tossed them three white aprons stained with tomato sauce and grease. Furlong put one on himself, tossed the other two to Bon Bon, and walked straight back into the kitchen.

"You're doing great," Bon Bon assured Lyra, reaching over and tying the apron on Lyra first. After they were both set, they trotted back to the kitchen. Furlong looked impatient. He tapped his hoof on the flour-dusted concrete floor. "I don't got all day, Drops."

Then Furlong did something quite odd. He quickly looked around, opened the fridge door, and stepped inside. Lyra and Bon Bon exchanged a look before doing the same. Chilly crates of tomatoes, mozzarella, and arugula surrounded them, but there was something strange about this room. Like it was meant for another purpose.

Soon, the floor was moving beneath

* ❋ * **31** * ❋ *

their hooves! It carried both the produce and the ponies deep into the ground below Manehattan. Light streamed through two small windows on the sides of the elevator as they passed each level.

DING!

The fridge door opened. Lyra and Bon Bon couldn't believe their eyes. There were over a hundred ponies, all wearing black and shuffling around the massive chrome-colored room. There were rows of desks, mysterious instruments and gadgets, and a massive sign on the back wall that said SECRET MONSTER INTELLIGENCE LEAGUE OF EQUESTRIA: MANEHATTAN BRANCH. WE'RE EVERYWHERE AND WE'RE NOWHERE.

Furlong coughed. "Welcome to the Manehattan Hidequarters of S.M.I.L.E., kids."

Chapter 5

S.M.I.L.E.

✦✦✦

Since Bon Bon and Agent Furlong had disa-
peared to discuss something in private, Lyra
was all alone for thirty minutes before a tall
mare with a curled yellow mane suddenly
extended her hoof. Her pink face was emo-
tionless. "You're the new agent, I take it.
Furlong told me to find you. He's busy at
the moment. Welcome to S.M.I.L.E. I'm

Alpha Hoof. I run things around here. Let me know if you need anything."

"Lyra Heartstrings," Lyra said, suddenly feeling shy. She extended her hoof and bumped it against Alpha's. "Thank you."

"You should get suited up with your hoofpack. Then meet us in the conference room for debriefing. This one's a doozy, so I hope your training is up to snuff, Agent Heartstrings." Alpha scoffed, and then her face became blank again. "See you soon."

Training? Suited up? Hoofpack? Lyra gulped. She surveyed the room for her friend or anything that might guide her. But Bon Bon was still nowhere to be found.

A pair of ponies wearing black vests and stern expressions trotted past, giving Lyra sidelong glances. The mare with an orange mane whispered something to the purple stallion. The stallion replied, "Absolutely, absolutely." The mare laughed, and the two ponies turned down the corridor.

"Excuse me." Lyra trotted over to an old mare with a graying mane and cat's-eye glasses. She was hunched over a typewriter, concentrating on transcribing a document. At the top it had been stamped with a red CLASSIFIED and a horseshoe symbol with two dots above it. "Do you know where Bon Bon—uh, I mean, Agent Sweetie Drops is?"

"Sorry, no," grumbled the old mare. She noticed Lyra staring at the document and put a folder on top of it protectively. "*Classified*, see?"

"Oh, I didn't mean to look—" Lyra was beginning to get anxious. How had she ended up here, in the subterranean depths of Manehattan? It was only a few hours ago that she and her best friend were back in Ponyville, recounting the Hearts and Hooves Day party over some frozen hot cocoa....

Lyra sighed, feeling lost and wishing she had some cocoa to soothe her right now. Then she got an idea. Where did everypony congregate in offices? The break room, of course! Lyra took off down the corridor where she had seen the two other ponies heading and hoped for the best.

As she trotted down the hall, Lyra peeked her head into each room. Every time another S.M.I.L.E. pony saw her, he or she closed the door. A few times, Lyra had managed a short glimpse inside. She was still trying to recover from the sight of an entire room filled with baby tatzlwurms and timberwolves in cages. She was wondering what other monsters were right under her muzzle when somepony called out to her.

"Agent Heartstrings?"

It took Lyra a moment to respond, still unaccustomed to hearing herself addressed as a secret agent. "Yes?" She turned around to face a sturdy white Earth pony stallion. He had a short, spiky aqua-colored mane and wore the standard black vest, hoof-watch, and black sunglasses. His cutie mark was a blue fox.

"I'm Foxtrot. Do you want to come meet the team?"

Lyra nodded and followed him into a nearby room. Compared to the other spaces in the snazzy hidequarters, the break room was quite simple. There were apples, drinks, and other refreshments displayed on the counter. A large seating area with tables populated the center. Music blared from a set of speakers.

The two ponies from earlier were at a table in the corner, drinking from paper cups. The mare with the orange mane was whispering to her friend. "I heard she has no experience! Why would Chief think we needed a wild card right now? Remember when he brought Sweetie Drops in?"

"*Look* how that turned out...." The purple stallion shook his blue mane. "I mean, look how *that* turned out." He made his eyes large, and the two sighed in unison.

Lyra took note of this odd behavior.

"Ahem!" Foxtrot said audibly. He raised his eyebrows at the other two. "This is our new recruit, Agent Heartstrings. This is Tango and Bravo."

"Oh!" said Tango as she sprang to her hooves, a slight blush forming upon her face. "Did you hear any of that?"

"I thought secret agents were supposed to be discreet...." Lyra teased. But nopony smiled. "Just joking...."

"We don't really joke," Bravo admitted with a shrug. The purple Unicorn looked to his comrades for backup. "Joking's just not our thing."

"But your organization is called S.M.I.L.E...." Lyra giggled.

"We never smile." Tango's face didn't break.

"Then maybe you should be called F.R.O.W.N. instead," Lyra replied with a smirk. She couldn't help making jokes. Perhaps she would fit in horribly here.

Tango made a funny face. "But then what would the Friendship Ranger Organization of Worldwide Neighgotiations be called?"

"Seriously!" Bravo agreed with an eye roll. *"Seriously."*

What? Lyra thought.

Bravo and Tango tossed their cups in the trash bin, leaving Lyra in their dust. As they left, Lyra thought she could hear her name in their whispers.

"What is the Friendship Ranger Organization...?" Lyra turned to Foxtrot and scratched her mint-green mane in confusion. "Should I know that?"

"Don't mind those two. You lived in Ponyville, right? Then I believe you know F.R.O.W.N. as the Princess of Friendship and her friends," Foxtrot replied. "Code names Purple Rose, White Lily, Orange Poppy, Pink

Petunia, Blue Begonia, and Yellow Daisy." Foxtrot trotted to the counter and poured two cups of frozen cocoa. He passed one to Lyra. "Collectively, we call them the Flower Rangers. We alert them when it's time for action, but they have no idea we exist!"

"Really?" Lyra exclaimed, taking a sip of the offering. "Yeah, I do know them." She was starting to put the pieces together. It made sense that Twilight Sparkle and the other ponies would be involved. They had saved Equestria on more than one occasion. But they were unwittingly working for S.M.I.L.E.? This was probably just the tip of the iceberg with all this secret-organization business. Her mind was officially blown.

"Yes, those amazing ponies are Equestria's real defense," Foxtrot said, beaming. "The dragon's in on it, too. Ever hear about what that little guy did in the Crystal Empire?"

"Saved the whole thing, right? Thanks for keeping me up to speed," Lyra replied. "Anything else I should know?"

"Breezies were a cover-up. Tirek was a cover-up. Don't even get me started on the escape-from-the-moon thing with Princess Luna. At least that one worked out pretty well. Except for the—" Foxtrot clapped his hoof over his mouth and laughed, cracking himself up at this joke.

"Hey! You smiled."

"Don't tell anypony," Foxtrot replied. "Now let's get going. There's a mission waiting with our names on it." Foxtrot turned on his hoof and headed out. "And wipe that grin off your face!"

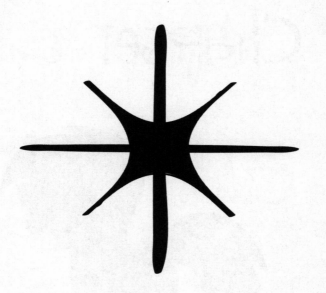

Chapter 6

Mission Given

★ ★ ★

"Now that we're all acquainted, we can get down to business." Agent Furlong shone a light from his horn onto the projector. It lit up the white wall with an array of colorful images. "You six have been selected to be part of a very special mission. Operation Swiss Cheese to be precise."

Furlong gestured to the wall. "These are the teams." There were three pairs of ponies depicted: Alpha Hoof and Bravo, Tango and Foxtrot, and last…Lyra and Bon Bon. Lyra smiled. Furlong frowned at her and grunted. "Each team will be going to a different location to investigate the recent reports of… changeling infestation." Furlong switched the pictures on the wall to a display of various changelings, a drawing of a massive changeling hive, and a menacing picture of Queen Chrysalis in the middle. The various changelings all looked the same—black Unicorn ponies with gauzy teal wings, glowing eyes, and legs riddled with holes. They hissed with their forked tongues shooting through their sharp fangs.

"The changelings are back?" Lyra yelled in shock, standing up. "The terrifying creatures who feed off love? When did this happen?" Everypony looked taken aback. Bon

Bon reached over and pulled Lyra back into her chair.

"Yes, Agent Heartstrings." Agent Furlong changed the projector slide. "I'm afraid so." It was a map of Equestria with scattered red dots. "Or at least we *think* so. We thought we had eradicated the problem after the royal wedding in Canterlot, but now word has reached us that we've still got work to do. We have no leads on where the hive is. Or *if* there is a hive."

"I assume Princess Celestia knows?" Foxtrot asked, nonchalant. He took a sip of his frozen cocoa. "Full disclosure?"

"Affirmative." Furlong nodded. He began pacing the front of the room. "Actually, it was the castle who informed us of these new changeling developments and reopened this branch of S.M.I.L.E. to combat them."

He tilted his head. "Well, that and some minor bugbear issues." He looked pointedly at Bon Bon. "Tartarus still needs work, kids. But we'll cross that bridge."

Bon Bon shrank into her seat. She was the one who had been at fault during the bugbear escape incident. The massive bee-bear hybrid monster had found its way out of Tartarus. It was the whole reason the agency in Canterlot was shuttered. Or so she thought....But she had never even known about this whole other hidequarters facility in Manehattan, so the agency was even more secretive than she realized. So many layers.

"What's with the red dots, Chief?" Tango nodded toward the map. "Don't tell me those are confirmed sightings!"

"We've got our work cut out for us," Bravo observed. "*Major* work cut out."

"Have you ever seen a changeling swarm forming? I have," Tango added. Lyra thought she saw a smirk forming on the yellow Pegasus's face. "It takes over the whole sky! One time, back when I first joined the force, it was so bad that—"

"Let's focus, everypony!" Alpha Hoof barked. She turned back to the map and gestured to Furlong. "Continue with the debriefing, Agent Furlong."

"Thank you, Alpha. These dots mark *possible* locations of the alleged changelings. But as you all know, *or you'd better know*"—Furlong looked at Lyra—"changelings' power lies in their ability to shape-shift. They could be anypony, and they could be anywhere.

"Your mission is simple—identify the changeling suspects and report to me. Then we'll call for reinforcements. As part of S.M.I.L.E., we take all precautions against being identified by these monsters or the civilians. We *cannot* be detected," Furlong urged everypony, slamming his hoof on the wooden table. "But if somepony *does* learn something they shouldn't know, you know what to do." Furlong pulled out his hoof mirror. "Reflection Deflection."

Bon Bon shuddered, thinking about how Furlong had almost erased Lyra's memory earlier with a Ref Def. Bon Bon had always disliked the memory-eraser spell. She counted herself lucky never to be the Unicorn in the pair, so she didn't have to do it directly. It didn't hurt ponies at all, of course. It was just a magic spell that made them forget certain classified things. It was a safety measure.

"Be careful with this, Agent Heartstrings," Furlong warned as he tossed the hoof mirror to Lyra. "The last two agents we tried out Deflected each other so much for sport that they couldn't remember what their mission was, the incompetent fools." Furlong shook his head in disbelief. "We had to dismiss Agent Flim and Agent Flam after a single day." The stallion grunted. "That's an agency record."

"Any news from those two?" Foxtrot asked. He furrowed his brow in genuine concern. "Where are they?"

"We have reason to believe they are stuck in Las Pegasus." Furlong shrugged. "But we have bigger apple fritters to fry today, kids."

"Let's not drag this out anymore, Chief,"

Alpha Hoof said, squirming in her seat. "Give us our assignments?"

"Alpha Hoof, Bravo—you're covering the Crystal Empire. Pay special attention to the royal couple, since they've attracted the changelings in the past. The Crystal Heart should be closely monitored. Lotta love in that place." The two ponies nodded their heads in understanding.

Furlong trotted over to the next pair. "Tango, Foxtrot—you two kids will be watching the Applewood region, aka home of the movies. Remember, this area can be tricky. Many ponies there may seem like changelings at first, but they could just be actors trying out different roles. Be triple sure if you call for alert."

Finally, Agent Furlong stopped in front of Lyra and Bon Bon. He put his hooves on the table and leaned over. "And you two will be stationed in Appleloosa. There have been some strange happenings down at a famous apple farm. That Farmer Apple Crispy needs a closer look. It will be hardest of all to blend in there, so I'll need you to be convincing. Are you up to the task?"

Lyra and Bon Bon looked at each other, filled with nerves and excitement. "We are," said Lyra, eager to get training in the field from her best friend. They were about to go on the greatest friendship adventure they'd ever had, even if it was a secret.

Chapter 7

Mares in Black

★ ★ ★

Agent Furlong led the pair of best friends through a series of secret doors, down a staircase, and into a hoofprint-protected room. It was full of items that looked like everyday objects but really did all sorts of other things. In this room, anything could be anything.

"I actually missed this," Bon Bon admitted. Her cerulean eyes sparkled with excitement as she scanned the massive room. There were horseshoes that emitted special smoke to aid in quick escapes. A glass case of quills that allowed the pony who wrote with them to magically write in different undetectable codes. And racks upon racks of disguises for undercover assignments.

"This is incredible!" Lyra marveled, riffling through a trunk of cowpony hats. "What do these do?"

"They go on your head, kid." Furlong snorted. "Now, let's get you two looking like Appleloosans."

Over the next hour, Lyra and Bon Bon were supplied with the latest gadgets in S.M.I.L.E. technology. In addition to the hoof mirrors, they were given watches with communication devices installed in them, a hoofpack of provisions, and new outfits.

"Good luck, kids." Furlong tipped his head toward them before departing.

"I thought we might wear the black vests that everypony else has on," Lyra commented as she inspected herself in a large mirror. "Aren't these a little over-the-top?" She ran her hoof along the brown fringe of her jacket and cowpony boots. A red hat and apple-print scarf finished the look.

"Not if we want to convince everypony we belong. Which is imperative to persuading a changeling to show its true form." Bon Bon stepped out of the changing room wearing a traditional green Appleloosan dress with puff sleeves. Lyra tried to stifle her giggles.

"Well, whatever you think is right....I trust you." Lyra met Bon Bon's eyes. "This is all so amazing, Bon Bon! I can't believe this was your life before you came to Ponyville."

"It's your life now, too." Bon Bon sounded sad. "I'm really sorry I dragged you into all this."

"I'm not! This is so exciting! Plus, we're best friends. There is nopony I would rather spend my time with than you," Lyra exclaimed with a huge smile. A brown mare with a gray mane nearby stopped inspecting a teakettle and frowned at her. Lyra stopped smiling. "Oops, I forgot. Must remain serious."

The two ponies laughed quietly.

"Hey, where did you go earlier?" Lyra asked, adjusting her apple scarf.

Bon Bon scrunched up her nose. "What?"

"With Agent Furlong? I was looking for you, and you just disappeared." Lyra nudged her friend. "You were gone a long time."

"Oh." Bon Bon stiffened. She turned to the mirror and fluffed her pink-and-blue mane. "It was nothing. He just needed my advice on something. It was—"

"Classified?" Lyra cut in. She raised a brow. "More secrets?"

"Something like that." Bon Bon grabbed her hoofpack. "But enough hanging around here at S.M.I.L.E. We have to go ... *now*."

"Why does this keep happening to me today?" Lyra teased. Bon Bon grabbed Lyra's hoof and pulled her out to the hallway. The two ponies barreled through the hidequarters. A short maze of silver halls and another cold elevator ride later, they were well on their way to Appleloosa to save Equestria. Operation Swiss Cheese was in full effect. Lyra just hoped there were no holes in the plan.

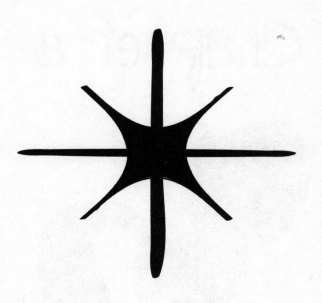

Chapter 8

Welcome to Appleloosa!

★ ★ ★

"Act natural," Bon Bon whispered as they disembarked onto the dusty wooden train platform. "Blend in while we get an idea of what's occurring in this place. Look for suspicious activity. Don't talk to anypony, okay?"

Lyra nodded her mint mane and followed

Bon Bon through the dusty terrain into the center of the Western town. The main street was lined with businesses on both sides, including a charming saloon called the Salt Block and a town hall. Sure enough, ponies dressed just like them—in cowpony hats, dresses, and fringe—trotted to and fro across the street.

"Nopony has noticed us, Bon Bon!" Lyra whispered, enchanted with everything about her current situation. "We're blending in!"

"Howdy there!" a gold stallion immediately called out.

"Or not," said Bon Bon, shooting Lyra an angry look.

"You're new here, and I'm Braeburn!" the stallion said as he trotted over. He wore a brown vest and cowpony hat, which looked great with his huge smile. "Welcome to beautiful Appleeee-loosa!" He kicked his forelegs up in the air. "What brings you fine ponyfolks here to our fair town?" The piece of hay in his mouth bobbed up and down as he spoke.

"I'm Sweetie, and this here is Heartstrings," Bon Bon said, curtsying in her green dress. She didn't miss a beat. "We're apple salesponies from a little town near Dodge Junction, and we're looking for a new supplier."

"Yee-haw, we heard that y'all got a great farmer in town here. Mr. Apple Crispy?" Lyra added with a drawl that sounded quite forced. "Hot diggety!"

"That's right, miss." Braeburn gave Lyra a funny look. "Appleloosa is indeed home to one famous Farmer Apple Crispy. I'd, uh...

introduce ya, but he's a little, uh ... *under the weather* right now." Braeburn's eyes darted around. He was definitely hiding something. "Can I interest you fillies in some delicious local Appleoosan applesauce at the Salt Block?"

Bon Bon and Lyra exchanged a look. The more time they spent in Braeburn's presence, the more clues he would have about them to piece together.

"I don't know, we best be gettin' to our barn-and-breakfast to check in...." Bon Bon said, even though Lyra was positive they had not made a reservation anywhere. "Beat the rush!"

"Is that what's got yer fringe in a twist?" Braeburn playfully nudged Bon Bon. "Why, you've got a-nothin' to worry about there!" Braeburn smiled. "We don't get many visitors down here in Appleloosa as is. Not since the rodeo ended, anyway."

Lyra perked up. "Is that so?"

"Sadly, yes." Braeburn's shoulders slumped. "Why, the last visitor we've had 'round was Granny Honeycomb's cousin Old Delilah! And she's been stayin' at the barn-and-breakfast so long, she's startin' to feel like family."

"And how long does that take?" asked Bon Bon.

"A few weeks or so." Braeburn chuckled. "So you're next!" He motioned down the road. "Say, there's Delilah now."

For an old mare, she was exceptionally stunning. Delilah had a beautiful gold-and-silver mane, a sky-blue hide, and a cutie mark of a gold heart-shaped apple. She wore a gold Appleloosan dress that shimmered in the sunlight. Lyra and Bon Bon were transfixed. Never before had they seen such a composed, exquisite mare. They watched as Old Delilah trotted along, stopping ponies as she passed and greeting them with warm words. Each time she moved on to another group, the ponies looked like they might faint with awe.

"Wow," breathed Bon Bon. "What a mare!"

"She is somethin'," Braeburn agreed, admiring her. He turned back to his new friends. "Now, how about that applesauce?"

"Sure! Why not?" Lyra sprang forward, taking the lead. Bon Bon looked shocked. Lyra wasn't following the plan! They were supposed to remain as anonymous as possible, per the S.M.I.L.E. code, not go around chatting to ponies in saloons, chomping on applesauce.

"Say, I'll catch up with you ponies in a tick," Bon Bon said. She stifled a very fake yawn. "I'm plum knackered."

"Suit yourself." Lyra shrugged and trotted off toward the Salt Block with Braeburn. Bon Bon was baffled. Clearly her best friend had an idea, but Bon Bon could not see how applesauce related to locating a changeling. It was beginning to look like Bon Bon would have to figure out this puzzle on her own.

Chapter 9

The update

✷ ✷ ✷

The sun peeked through the gauzy white curtains of Bon Bon's room at the barn-and-breakfast. Bon Bon stretched her hooves up above her head with a yawn and tried to think of the day's plan, when her watch communicator began to flash red and green. Her stomach dropped. It was Agent Furlong, looking for an update. And they had *nothing*.

While Lyra had been at the Salt Block distracting Braeburn last night, Bon Bon had taken the chance to snoop around town. It was less conspicuous by herself actually. She could do more slinking and hiding. But after a few hours, the only information that Bon Bon had gathered was that Sheriff Silverstar liked to nap on the job and that there was a Saddle Hawkins square dance coming up.

Bon Bon tapped the watch. "Hello, Chief."

"Agent Drops, I got your report about the farm visit you and your partner are going on today." His voice came in scratchy.

What? thought Bon Bon. *I didn't send a report.*

"Keep up the good work. And let me know if our suspicions are confirmed about Farmer Crispy ASAP."

"Copy," Bon Bon replied, puzzled.

"Furlong, over and out." The scratchy noise came to a stop, and the watch blinked off. Bon Bon looked over at Lyra in the bed across the room. She was snoring softly, and her rumpled mint-and-white mane stuck out in every direction.

"Agent Heartstrings!" Bon Bon called out. "Wake up!"

Lyra sprang out of bed, rubbing her golden eyes awake. "Reporting for duty!"

"Wow, you're taking this thing really seriously," Bon Bon marveled. "Did you report to Agent Furlong with my communicator?"

"Maaaaybe?" Lyra smiled like a little filly on Hearth's Warming Eve. "I didn't want to steal your thunder, but I talked Braeburn into taking us to the farm. And even he said there's something very strange about the way Farmer Apple Crispy has been acting."

Bon Bon stood up. "What do you mean?"

"Braeburn said that the apples aren't growing and the farm is a mess! It's like he's *forgotten* how to farm," Lyra said, eyes growing wide. "Almost like . . . he isn't himself."

Bon Bon gasped. "Let's go find out if we've got a changeling on our hooves."

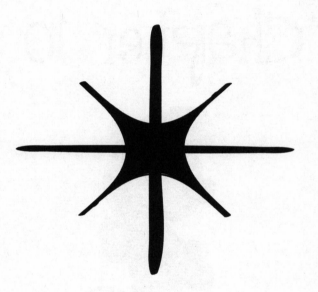

Chapter 10

Farmer Apple Crispy's Farm

★ ★ ★

The fields were overgrown, and the apples were beginning to rot. There was an odd stench in the air, baking in the hot Apple-loosan afternoon sun. No crops had been plowed, and no trees had been bucked in the past few weeks, which everypony knew was long enough to let things go awry on a farm.

Braeburn kicked a rotting Jonagold with his hoof and sighed. "We tried to help him out, of course!" Braeburn said, full of despair. "But Farmer Apple Crispy told us to get on and scram, too. He said he's got no interest in apple farmin' anymore and wanted us off his property."

"Why would he say such a thing?" Lyra asked. "Doesn't he provide a big portion of the apples for the town?"

"That's right," Braeburn replied. "In fact, Farmer Apple Crispy was supposed to supply the food for the Saddle Hawkins square dance tonight." He took off his cowpony hat and rubbed his mane, giving himself an unkempt look. It mirrored the appearance of the dilapidated farm they stood on. "I don't even want to break the news to the townsponies that there won't be any Apple Crispy apple crisp to munch on."

"How awful," Lyra said, putting her mint hoof on Braeburn to comfort him. "Farmer Crispy must be real sick, huh?"

"Maybe he's not sick at all...." said Bon Bon, scribbling some notes on a scroll. She was starting to recognize the telltale signs of a changeling: the pony in question was acting completely different than usual, he didn't seem to care for the well-being of other ponies, and he didn't mind not having food to eat. Changelings didn't need to eat because they fed off love! Bon Bon was feeling more certain by the minute that Farmer Apple Crispy had been replaced.

"Has anypony else in town been acting strange?" Bon Bon queried. She began to pace as she thought.

Braeburn shook his head. "No, ma'am, but I've noticed everypony lookin' real tired. Even me." Braeburn's eyes grew wide as he made a realization. "Oh no! You don't think we're all gettin' sick, too?"

Tired ponies... thought Bon Bon. *Ponies get tired when they have the love sucked out of them.* They had definitely found what they were looking for. Bon Bon was ready to report their discoveries to Furlong and bring Operation Swiss Cheese to a swift and triumphant close.

"No, no. I'm sure you're not sick. But do ya mind if Heartstrings and I try and help him?" said Bon Bon, anxiously regarding the farmhouse. "We may have a way to make him feel better."

"Be my guest." Braeburn shrugged. "I'll be humdinged if ya can get any further than I did." Braeburn tipped his hat and trotted off to go help set up the square dance.

As soon as he was a safe distance away, Bon Bon cantered right to the front door of the farmhouse, filled with a mixture of confidence and anticipation. Maybe she wouldn't even call for F.R.O.W.N. backup like she was supposed to. She and Lyra could vanquish the changeling on their own! Then maybe Tango, Bravo, and the other S.M.I.L.E. agents would respect her again after her mess-up in Tartarus...not to mention she'd get her part of the secret bargain she'd made with Furlong back at the hidequarters. Everything was going perfectly.

Bon Bon lifted her hoof and was about

to knock when a rotten apple hit her square in the head. "Ow!"

"Pssst!" Lyra hissed from the bushes. She was crouched and hidden, but her red hat made it hard for her to blend in with the foliage. "What are you doing, Bon Bon?"

"I'm going to defeat the changeling!" Bon Bon whispered back. "Or at least reason with it." Lyra sprang from the bushes, galloped over, and pulled Bon Bon back into hiding with her.

"No, you're not. You're being ridiculous, Agent Sweetie Drops!" Lyra whispered, a hint of annoyance in her voice. "Didn't you listen to the debriefing back at hidequarters? Agent Furlong said we're not *supposed* to make a big commotion. We're just supposed to be sure that he really is a changeling!" Lyra raised her brow. "Shouldn't we, you know... *wait* and observe Farmer Apple Crispy for a while? See if what he does is... changeling-y?"

Bon Bon rolled her eyes. "I've been a part of the squad for much longer than you, Lyra. Which makes me the senior member of this team, so I think we should go over and—"

"Shhh!" Lyra put her hoof against Bon Bon's mouth and pointed to the red picket-fence front gate of the farm. "Look!" It was none other than Old Delilah, looking pleased with herself, trotting to the front door. In her right hoof was a basket of fresh apple fritters tied with a bow.

Delilah hummed a jaunty tune as she knocked on the door. She fluffed her silver-and-gold mane, which was pinned into an updo. When the door opened, Farmer

Apple Crispy almost melted into a puddle. "Mah sweet Delilah!" the scruffy old farmer cried out. He placed his hoof to his heart. "It's felt like an eternity since I saw ya last."

"My dear Crispy!" she replied with a smile. "I've missed you, too! I've brought ya these apple fritters and come here with a mind to asking ya to the Saddle Hawkins square dance." She batted her long eyelashes. "That is, if you'll have me."

"Of course I will!" Apple Crispy grinned, a silly look in his green eyes. A look that was so undeniable, even Bon Bon could admit she'd been wrong about the whole thing.

"I don't believe it...." Bon Bon's jaw dropped. "Farmer Apple Crispy is not a changeling...he's in *love*!"

Chapter 11

glowing for It
★ ★ ★

"There is nothin' that would make me happier than to swing ya around to the beat of a two-step, mah darlin'." Farmer Crispy leaned in and nuzzled Old Delilah, knocking off his straw hat in the process. But he didn't care.

She held him close, resting her head upon Farmer Crispy's shoulder so that her face was still visible to Lyra. Delilah's expression was strange. She was smiling but stiff. A moment later, Delilah's eyes began to glow a neon blue color!

"Bon Bon, look!" Lyra whispered. "That's not normal."

"Sure, it is," Bon Bon replied in disbelief. "But not for a pony...."

Delilah smirked as she pulled away from Apple Crispy. He slumped down, exhausted. "Are you all right, Crispy?" she said sweetly. "You look mighty tired. Shall I come back later?"

"Yeah, yeah. Good idea...." The pony farmer barely managed to speak the words before collapsing into an exhausted heap on the front porch. He began to snore.

Delilah smiled. She wasn't surprised at this development in the slightest! The mare proceeded to pick up her basket of fritters and trot off back down toward town, humming the same tune as before. As soon as she was gone, Lyra and Bon Bon burst from the bushes. "Delilah is the changeling!" they said in unison.

"We have to alert Agent Furlong immediately!" Lyra called out, galloping after Bon Bon. At that moment, Bon Bon realized her best friend was right, there was no way they could take on a changeling by themselves. They had to follow orders.

The two ponies ducked around the back corner of a building, and Bon Bon took out her communicator watch. Lyra watched her friend as she tapped the face with her hoof, and it lit up green and red. "Message to Agent Furlong," Bon Bon barked. "Are you there?"

The watch blinked and buzzed for ages,

but there was no response. Bon Bon let out a frustrated grunt and tried another series of buttons. "Message to Operation Swiss Cheese. Special Agent Sweetie Drops, Appleloosa Unit, here. THE HOLES ARE IN THE CHEESE. *I REPEAT: THE HOLES ARE IN THE CHEESE.*" The watch made a scratchy noise, which according to Agent Furlong meant somepony was listening. "One more thing—there is a square dance here tonight. Potential love in the air. Agent Drops, over and out."

Bon Bon seemed unsatisfied. She turned to Lyra. "We can try again later, but that will have to do for now. Maybe Foxtrot or Bravo will hear it. They usually respond to communications."

"What if nopony shows up to help us?" Lyra asked, biting her lip in concern.

Bon Bon whimpered. "Then I guess you and I might have to fight a changeling on our own." How had they gone from their life in Ponyville to this? Bon Bon almost couldn't believe it.

"Whatever happens," Lyra said, reaching her hoof out, "we'll be by each other's side, right?"

Bon Bon reached her hoof out and met Lyra's. "Right."

Chapter 12

It's Element-ary, Dear Bon Bon

★ ★ ★

A few hours later, there were still no responses from anypony else from Operation Swiss Cheese. So Bon Bon and Lyra busied themselves with preparing for the Saddle Hawkins square dance as if it were a big exam in school. But they didn't practice their hoofsteps. Instead, Lyra sat in their barn-and-breakfast room, hunched over a book on changelings that Agent Furlong had left in her hoofpack. Every so often, the Unicorn would make a grunting noise and scribble something down on her scroll. Bon Bon kept trying to call Agent Furlong, wondering if there might be some worse infestation in the Crystal Empire or in Applewood that he was tending to instead.

"Did you know that if surrounded by too much love at once, hungry changelings can no longer hold their disguised form?" Lyra asked Bon Bon. The latter was pacing the room in the most grating fashion.

"Of course I know that," Bon Bon snapped, looking at her watch.

"They go into something called a feeding

frenzy," Lyra continued. "They can't help roaring and hissing!"

Bon Bon let out a small chuckle at her friend's enthusiasm. Who knew that Lyra could get so into S.M.I.L.E. trivia? It was still strange to have her be a part of this life, but Bon Bon had to admit Lyra was taking to it like a fish to water.

"She's right, you know." A familiar stallion's voice from behind the door startled them. Bon Bon trotted to the door and looked through the peephole to be sure. "Agent Bravo!" she exclaimed. "Why are you here?" Bon Bon unlocked the latch on the door and let the pony in.

"Got your message," Bravo replied with a smile. "Agent Furlong sent me to tell you that your mission is done. Please return."

"What?" Lyra stood up, causing her book to fall to the floor. "What about the changeling we found here?"

"It shall be dealt with," Bravo answered robotically. "Please report back."

Bon Bon shrugged and looked to the distraught Lyra. "Chief's orders are Chief's orders." Then Bon Bon grabbed her hoof-pack and began to toss items into it. Lyra didn't budge. She kept staring at Bravo like he'd just come back from a trip to the moon.

"Like it or not, Lyra, we have to go," Bon Bon advised. When her Unicorn friend didn't budge, Bon Bon let out a heavy sigh. Why didn't she ever follow directions?

"Do we?" Lyra's eyes narrowed as she stared down Bravo. "I'm not sure we do."

There was something weird about Bravo. Ever since Lyra had stepped hoof in the hidequarters at S.M.I.L.E., he'd been rude and dismissive to her. In the break room, Bravo had kept whispering to Tango, and during debriefing, he had made tons of faces when he thought Lyra wasn't looking. Lyra had decided she didn't like Bravo for these reasons. But she had absolutely no feelings about the pony standing in front of them now because it wasn't him. Sure, he looked like the same Unicorn, with his light purple hide and short blue mane. But Lyra was sure of it. This Bravo was an imposter!

Lyra trotted over to "Bravo" and looked into his blue eyes, searching for a faint glow in them. But nothing happened. "May I have a private word with my best friend?" she asked.

"Sure," Bravo replied with a friendly smile.

"We'll meet you at the train station in fif-teen minutes," Bon Bon told the stallion. He nodded and trotted out of the room. Lyra watched him leave the barn-and-breakfast from the window to make sure he was really gone before she told Bon Bon.

"He's a changeling," Lyra observed. "I don't know if he's the same one as Delilah or a completely new one. But he's definitely a changeling!"

"What?" Bon Bon scoffed. "Just because you found one changeling and read a book about them does not mean *everypony* is a changeling!"

"He wasn't acting like himself," Lyra insisted. She put a hoof on Bon Bon's shoul-der and then pointed it to Bon Bon's pink-and-blue mane. "Think about it, Bon Bon!"

"I've known Bravo a long time," Bon Bon

sassed back. "He's not the warmest pony in Equestria, I know. But that was him."

"You're missing something...." Lyra smiled. "Bravo always says everything twice!" Lyra threw her hooves into the air in excitement. "And that pony only said things once. *And* he smiled! Bravo never smiles!" She knew she had it right. The changeling didn't know these quirks about the pony it was trying to be.

But instead of congratulating Lyra on her stunning observations, Bon Bon was annoyed. Why was her best friend so good as this? Bon Bon was supposed to be the secret agent. "Lyra, why do you have to be such a know-it-all? I brought you into this organization so I could save you from the Reflection Deflection spell! So you could remember our friendship." Bon Bon threw her last few items into her hoofpack and tossed it over her shoulder. She trotted to the door. "But it seems you've forgotten it anyway. Are you a changeling that's replaced my best friend?"

"Bon Bon, wait—" Lyra begged. She hadn't meant to upset her friend. Lyra was just trying to help!

"Good luck with all your 'changelings,' Agent Heartstrings," Bon Bon said as she stood in the doorway. "Over and out."

Chapter 13

The Setup

★ ★ ★

Even though Lyra felt confused and upset by her argument with Bon Bon, she couldn't bring herself to leave the ponies of Apple-loosa with at least one confirmed changeling (and perhaps more) in their midst. Lyra was going to do everything in her power to help them, just as she'd promised Agent Furlong back in Manehattan.

And Lyra had a plan.

Time was already running out, so Lyra put on her Appleloosan getup and trotted over to the town dance hall, where tonight's festivities were going to take place. Lyra knew where to find it because Braeburn had pointed it out to her on his tour after they'd had applesauce the previous night.

When Braeburn had mentioned that the Appleloosans often held both "Wild West" dances and "Mild West" dances, Lyra asked which his cousin Applejack preferred. Then she had casually slipped into conversation that he should invite Applejack, along with her friends. Lyra had her hooves crossed that they would show up. Without Bon Bon, she was on her own and could use all the help she could get.

"Braeburn!" Lyra called out to the

stallion with a wave. He was at the top of a ladder, hanging some string lights above the dance floor. "The barn looks great! Perfect for a 'Wild West' dance, just as Applejack likes."

"Howdy, Heartstrings!" Braeburn hollered back. "And thank you!" He hopped down and trotted over. "Say...what's that in yer hooves, ma'am?"

"Oh, these?" Lyra looked down at the basket she was holding. It was full of red paper shaped like hearts. "These are just some extra Hearts and Hooves Day cards I had left over. I thought it would be nice if each pony gave one to somepony that they wanted to dance with at the Saddle Hawkins square dance." Lyra smiled. "You know, to spread the *love*."

"How creative." Braeburn grinned. He

picked up a Hearts and Hooves Day card and passed it back to Lyra. "Just like that?"

"Just like that." Lyra winked and passed him the basket. *The more love in this room, the better*, she thought. *It'll be a changeling's dream come true.* She turned on her hoof to leave the barn and then remembered one last detail.

"Have ya seen Delilah lately?" Lyra asked. "Is she still comin' tonight?"

"Oh, I reckon she wouldn't miss it for anythin'," Braeburn said with a tip of his hat. "See ya later, Ms. Heartstrings."

The sun was setting over Appleloosa, and almost everypony in town was trotting over to the big dance. Lyra took a moment to watch the sky darken and the stars blink to life. She was nervous. Lyra wondered what she could have done differently with Bon Bon and why her friend had been so touchy. This whole adventure was supposed to be about the two of them together! At first, Lyra had felt so special that Bon Bon was finally including her in the double life she once led.

"Lyraaaa!" she heard her name being called in the distance. She saw a pony galloping toward her but could only make out a silhouette. "Lyra!" Nopony here called her that, except...

"Bon Bon? Is that you?" Lyra exclaimed as her friend arrived, rumpled and out of breath. "What are you doing back here?"

"You were right, Lyra," Bon Bon admitted, shaking her head. "I wasn't paying attention to details like you were. I was so caught up with being the expert that I forgot to trust my best friend."

"What happened?" Lyra prodded. She tried hard not to appear smug.

"I watched Bravo board the train back to Manehattan, but as soon as I got on, he was nowhere to be found!" Bon Bon threw her hooves in the air. "That's when I knew that he never *was* Bravo. And he *does* say everything twice. I was being tricked by a changeling, just as you had figured out." Bon Bon frowned. "He was trying to get rid of us so we couldn't sabotage their plans to feed on the love tonight. I feel like such a rotten apple for ever doubting you."

"Don't worry." Lyra's face broke into a grin. "I forgive you, Bon Bon."

Bon Bon smiled, her cerulean eyes beginning to tear up. "You do?"

"Best friends forever, remember?" Lyra leaned over and hugged her buddy. "No amount of secret agenting is going to get in the way of that."

"Awww, isn't that precious?" a pony's voice interrupted, having noticed their embrace. "Two friends who love each other so very much!"

The ponies froze. It was nopony other than Delilah.

"Well, I best be gettin' on to that dance," Delilah said with a curtsy. "My honey awaits." As she trotted away, her eyes flashed blue again. Lyra and Bon Bon both shuddered. It had been too close of a call for comfort.

Chapter 14

The Saddle Hawkins Square Dance

★ ★ ★

As the ponies of the band started their set, strumming their fiddles and stomping their hooves, Lyra and Bon Bon surveyed the room. They kept a close eye on Delilah, who was making the rounds saying hello to everypony. The gorgeous old mare clung to Farmer Apple Crispy's hoof, and the stallion looked quite proud of himself for it. But the astonishment that registered on the townsponies' faces at the new "it couple" of Appleloosa would be short-lived, replaced by another breed of the same emotion soon. Bon Bon felt a little bad for Farmer Crispy, even if it was for his own good.

"Swing yer partner 'round and 'round... stomp yer hooves, and yell real loud!" the pony up front called out to the dancers in the center. The stallions and mares followed each of his instructions dutifully, forming elaborate patterns with their colorful hooves and dresses. "A right and left around the ring...while the roosters crow and the birdies sing!"

Lyra noticed a mare across the room

giving a stallion one of the Hearts and Hooves Day cards. He read and began to blush. Delilah, who watched with curious interest, started to twitch. She then turned her attention to the cider table, where a couple of old stallion buddies shared a funny story from their colt days. They clinked their ciders in good cheer and put a friendly hoof around each other, swaying to the music. Delilah's twitching became more pronounced.

Lyra nudged Bon Bon. "Look! I think she's gonna go into a frenzy...."

"You're right," Bon Bon agreed. "Almost time now."

The caller pony bellowed to the dancers in time to the beat. "Dog in the corner chewin' on a bone...meet yer filly, promenade her home!" The dancing mares giggled in delight as their partners swung them around the barn. At the sound of their laughter, Delilah's forked tongue started to dart out of her mouth. She struggled to keep it closed.

"Are ya all right, mah apple pie?" Farmer Crispy asked. His face contorted into worry. "Ya look a bit...strange."

"I'm, I'm..." Delilah tried to respond, but her words transformed into a loud hissing sound. Her eyes began to glow blue....

POP!

The music came to a screeching halt, and the caller pony's jaw dropped to the floor. In the place where Old Delilah had been, now stood a black insectlike pony creature with translucent wings, legs with holes in them, and sharp fangs! Its tongue darted out every which way.

POP! POP!

Two more changelings in the barn revealed themselves like kernels of popcorn. Now there were three hissing creatures, looking to suck the love out of everypony and ruin the night. One changeling sent a zap of green magic to one corner, burning a hole in the barn.

"Ahhhh!" The partygoers were scrambling toward the edges of the barn. "Help!"

Suddenly, a group of six ponies appeared at the barn door.

"Did we come at a bad time or something?" Rainbow Dash joked as she took off straight toward a changeling. "I gotta say, when you said *dance*, I was not expecting this!"

Bon Bon and Lyra exchanged excited looks. The plan was working!

"Feeding-frenzy time? Not on my watch." Twilight Sparkle spread her wings and aimed her horn at the Delilah changeling, sending a zap of purple magic. The changeling weakened slightly but flew toward a pony couple huddling together under the drinks table.

"Hey! That's not *nice!*" exclaimed Fluttershy, blocking the changeling's path. She held her ground and gave it the Stare. The changeling cowered.

Next, Pinkie Pie rolled her party cannon over to the wall. She jumped inside and launched herself along with her confetti straight at the third changeling, knocking it to the barn floor. "Wheeeee!" she squealed. "Changeling bowling!"

"I really didn't dress for a *changeling battle*, you know?" Rarity sighed and looked down at her over-the-top, glittery Appleloosan-style dress. "But never fear, I shall protect you ponies!" Then Rarity ripped the trim of lace off her hem, fashioned it into a lasso, and tossed it to Applejack, who caught the lasso in her mouth and swung it high over her head.

"Thanks, darling."

"Yee-haaaaaw!" Applejack shouted, tossing it around the three changelings in a single motion. The lasso tightened, tying them into a neat bundle on the center of the dance floor.

"Welcome to Appleloooooosa!" Braeburn said, voice wavering. "We sure do appreciate yer visit."

"Don't worry, Furlong will take care of the rest," whispered Bon Bon. Lyra nodded. She knew it was time to go. The two agents hoof-bumped each other, nodded, and stole away into the night. They were satisfied with a job well done, as best friends and excellent secret agent partners.

"Whoo-ee!" Applejack exclaimed, trotting up to her cousin. "It was real lucky ya had the idea to invite me and my friends to Appleloosa for the big square dance, wasn't it, Braeburn?"

"It was actually a pair o' ponies just passing through town who had the thought to do it," Braeburn replied, still looking shocked.

"What are their names, darling?" Rarity asked, brushing some dust off her gown. It was still almost in perfect shape despite all the action. "I am quite curious."

Braeburn turned around, scanning the crowd for where he'd last seen them. But all he saw were Appleloosans. But what did those two ponies look like again? "You know, I can't remember...."

"Hmmm, those names don't ring any of *my* bells...." said Pinkie Pie, picking up several hoofbells and ringing them one at a time. She shrugged. "But we do know lots of ponies."

"Well, whoever they were, they certainly helped us out," Twilight Sparkle added with a nod.

"That poor Farmer Apple Crispy," Fluttershy said as she trotted up, looking exhausted.

"Yeah, we got him back home, but I think it could be a while before he isn't shocked by the fact that his *girlfriend* was a *changeling*!" Rainbow Dash added.

The band, who couldn't remember why they'd stopped playing in the first place, struck up a new tune. Everypony joined in. Even Farmer Apple Crispy.

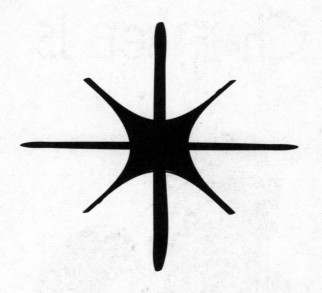

Chapter 15

The Deal

✦ ✦ ✦

The fireplace made the whole cottage glow with warmth and light. Bon Bon was in the kitchen making hot cocoa, while Lyra sat on the sofa working very hard on a new friendship bracelet project. It was gloriously uneventful.

"Here ya go, *Agent Heartstrings*," Bon Bon teased as she passed over the steaming mug.

"Thank you, *Agent Sweetie Drops*," she replied with a giggle as she took a sip of the delicious warm cocoa. The two ponies sat side by side as they sipped from their mugs, watching the snow falling gently outside the window.

"Hey, Bon Bon?"

"Yes, Lyra?"

"Why did Agent Furlong let us come back to Ponyville?"

"Because I Ref Def'd him."

Lyra's eyes grew enormous. "You didn't!"

Bon Bon laughed. "*Or*...because I made him a deal that he could call upon us for a mission whenever he wanted if he let us stay here in Ponyville with our friends." Bon Bon grinned. "But I told him we only work as a team. Is that okay with you?"

"I wouldn't have it any other way." Lyra smiled back, proudly this time. As far as she was concerned, there was no reason to ever hide it again.

Read them all!

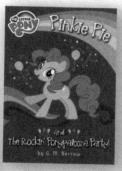

Turn the page for
a special surprise from
Lyra and Bon Bon!

SECRET MONSTER INTELLiGENCE LEAGUE OF EQUESTRIA (S.M.I.L.E.)

* * * * * * * *

[CONFIDENTIAL]

To reader:

We made these activity pages just for you. Please be sure to obtain security clearance before sharing with another agent.

Agent Drops * Agent Heartstrings

PICK YOUR PARTNER

Lyra and Bon Bon are lucky! Not only are they best friends, but they get to be partners in Equestria's top secret monster-fighting agency. If you were a member of S.M.I.L.E., who would you want to be your partner? Write about what makes this agent such a good teammate.

_____

_____

_____

_____

_____

_____

_____

_____

_____

_____

_____

_____

Top Secret Headquarters

The Manehattan branch of S.M.I.L.E. is hidden below Hay's Pizza. Can you help Lyra and Bon Bon find their way to the restaurant?

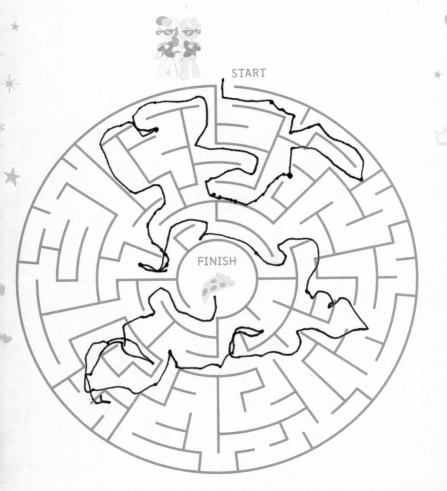

START

FINISH

FIELD NOTES

Good agents must be aware of their surroundings.
Use your observation skills to spot six differences
between these two ponies.

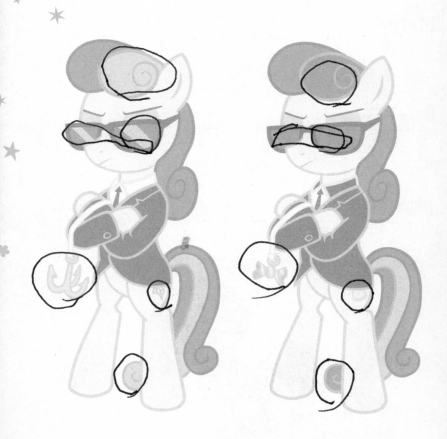

Mission: Possible

Agent Furlong has a new mission for Lyra and Bon Bon. Write the briefing in the space below. Don't forget to include any special instructions needed to ensure success!

Location:

Subject:

Directive:

SPECIAL INSTRUCTIONS:

_____

_____

_____

_____

_____

_____

_____

_____

_____

DEPARTMENT OF DISGUISES

Lyra and Bon Bon have no trouble at all fitting in with the Appleloosan ponies, but what would happen if their mission required them to wear disguises? Draw different looks on the ponies below so they can stay undercover.

CRACK THE CODE

Lyra and Bon Bon have found a secret message! Use the key below to decode the message!

A B C D E F G

H I J K L M N

O P Q R S T U

V W X Y Z

"keep up the good work the fate of equestria depends on you"

—Agent Furlong

THE NEXT LEVEL

Use what you've learned on the previous page to create your own code! First come up with a key. Then write a secret message on the following page!

TEAMWORK

Under cover in Appleloosa, Lyra and Bon Bon's friendship is tested when they disagree over the identity of a changeling. Have you ever had a fight with a friend while working on an important project? How did it make you feel? What did you do to resolve your differences?